ZOO SCHOOL

For **MPRPS** –

thanks for the inspiration!

Scholastic Press
An imprint of Scholastic Australia Pty Limited (ABN 11 000 614 577)
PO Box 579 Gosford NSW 2250
www.scholastic.com.au

Part of the Scholastic Group
Sydney • Auckland • New York • Toronto • London • Mexico City
• New Delhi • Hong Kong • Buenos Aires • Puerto Rico

First published by Scholastic Australia in 2020.
This edition published in 2023.

NATIONAL LIBRARY OF AUSTRALIA
A catalogue record for this book is available from the National Library of Australia

ISBN: 978-1-76026-446-8

Typeset in ITC Esprit, featuring Joppa.

Printed in China by Ink Asia.
Scholastic Australia's policy, in association with Ink Asia, is to use papers that are renewable and made efficiently from wood grown in responsibly managed forests, so as to minimise its environmental footprint.

10 9 8 7 6 5 4 3 24 25 26 27 / 2

Chameleon is hiding 16 times inside this book. Can you find him?

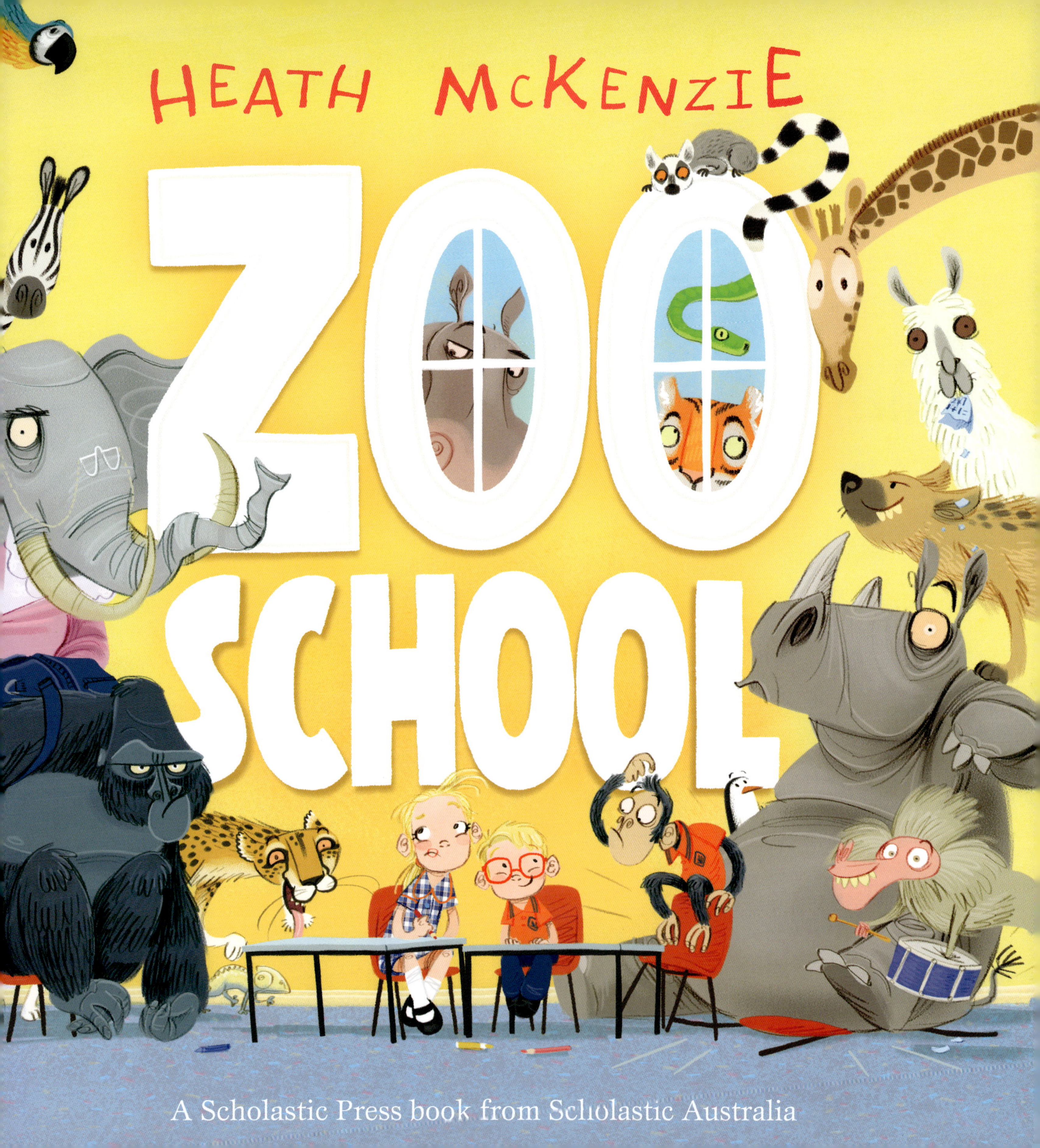
HEATH McKENZIE
ZOO
SCHOOL
A Scholastic Press book from Scholastic Australia

One morning young Oscar

was slow to get dressed.

His big sister Ava was

getting

quite

stressed!

MOO!
ZOO HOUSE

It was past nine o'clock!

They were running quite late!

So late, neither noticed

the broken

school

gate . . .

They **hung** up their bags, into class they **slunk**,

then noticed the teacher had grown . . .

. . . A LONG TRUNK!

Plus a pair of huge tusks
and two big, flappy ears!
And let's not even mention the

SIZEABLE
REAR!

Ch Monitors

But that wasn't all, for in Sophie's seat,

was a rather large silverback

picking its

feet!

Then out in the hall – a zebra STAMPEDE!

Which made silent reading time tricky indeed!

The music room thundered with rowdy **baboons**,
BANGING and **BLURTING** on drums and bassoons!

BLURT!

The gym was a madhouse of llamas and lemurs!

Vaulting and bouncing and hurdling with streamers!

The playground was **jam-packed** with
too many **creatures**,
so we went in search of one of our **teachers**!

We marched to the staffroom –

THIS JUST WASN'T FAIR!

But oddly, there seemed to be nobody there!

So it was up to us to sort out this bungle.

We'd have to decide who was

KING

of this jungle!

But how to decide?

What would be fair?

A maths test?

A fun run?

A bake off?

A DARE?!

No-one could agree on any one thing.

Then just as it all got too much, we heard . . .

DING!
DING!

The **end-of-day bell!** No more time for debating.
We all grabbed our bags, the grown-ups were **waiting!**

'We'll see you tomorrow!' we happily smiled.

'How was your day?' asked our mum.

'It was WILD!'